The Clan Book

Box Series, Books 1-3

By: Lea Larsen

Lea Larsen

© 2016

Printed in USA

Published by Lea Larsen

Cover Image: Produced by
Lea Larsen

© Copyright 2015

ISBN-
ISBN-

All Rights Reserved
No part of this publication may be reproduced or transmitted in any form whatsoever, electronic, or mechanical, including photocopying, recording, or by any informational storage or retrieval system without express written, dated and signed permission from the author.

By reading this you accept these terms and conditions.

TABLE OF CONTENTS

The Clan Book 1 1

The Clan Book 2 33

The Dragon's Mate: The Clan Book 3 68

The Dragon's Captive:

The Clan Book 1

By:Lea Larsen

© 2016

Table of Contents

Chapter one   3

Chapter Two   12

Chapter Three   20

Chapter Four   25

Chapter one

This was not her scene.

Alana Morgan sat at the bar as the dozens of drunk and sweaty patrons pressed in around her. Gyrating and grinding to the rhythm of annoyingly monotone club music that made it almost impossible to hear herself think. Let alone talk.

Alana knew she shouldn't have come. But, she'd had nothing else to do. She was tired of sitting in her dormitory every night while her roommate and the other girls from her floor went out on the town. She was tired of reading books or watching movies while eating falafel out of a sad, lonely takeout container.

So, when her roommate said that it was her friend's birthday and a bunch of them were going to a club called The Dragon's Lair, Alana had asked if she could tag along. Now, of course, her roommate had taken off to dance with some sleazy looking guy from the bar. The other girls they'd come with had done the same. And, Alana was now sitting at the bar. Alone.

If she'd known she was going to be feeling lonely anyway, she would have made the decision to stay behind in the dormitory after all. At least there she had falafel and her fantasy books to comfort her. Here, there was nothing. Nothing but awkward looks from strangers and the occasional leer from a drunken man across the bar.

Two of these guys had offered to buy her a drink and

one of them had asked her to dance. She declined all offers.

Honestly, she knew she should, at the very least, make an effort. But, all the men who seemed interested in her gave her a definite creepy, potential rapist vibe. Not to mention, none of them was her physical type at all.

Every man who had come up to her were either the types who wore baggy pants, gold chains, and gold teeth or sported what Alana called 'the serial killer comb-over'.

Not that there weren't good looking guys in this club. Truth be told, she'd been eying the ripped redhead across the bar for almost an hour. Hoping that he might catch her gaze and come over.

Unfortunately, he seemed more interested in watching his companion strike out with pairs of girls who looked, to Alana at least, like super models.

She watched the redhead smile slightly as his friend, a short, skinny guy with longish brown hair, get rejected by a couple of (what Alana assumed to be) blonde twin sisters.

She couldn't help but be amused by the little brown haired guys attempts. Clearly he didn't know that the girls he was going after were out of his league.

That, Alana, guessed was why the creepy guys went for her instead of the supermodels. They figured she was the safer bet.

Not that she was bad looking at all. She was proportional, of average height and her bright blue eyes earned her many a compliment. But, with a few freckles still on her nose (even at the age of nineteen) and a tiny hint of baby fat still in her cheeks, she gave off more of a girl next door vibe than a victoria's secret model one.

And, in her limited experience with clubs like this one, guys didn't go after the hottest looking girl in the place. They went after the best-looking girl they thought they had a chance with.

But men like the red head, with his on point hair cut, chiseled features, and well-defined abs, which were displayed nicely in his too tight white shirt, could get any girl they wanted. Alana was sure that, if he tried, he could have the girls his little friend was going after eating out of the palm of his hand. Despite that, he seemed completely uninterested.

Alana couldn't help but wonder why that was. She sipped on the southern comfort she had ordered and leaned over to watch him a bit more closely. When he turned his eyes to her, she felt an embarrassed flush creep up her face. Her mind began to frantically search for other places to look. Places that would make it look like she wasn't staring at him.

Then he smiled at her. Her heart started pounding in her chest as he raised his drink in her direction. She felt it speed up as she watched him stand from his stool and make his way around the bar.

When he stopped in front of her, she found that she could hardly breathe.

"Hi," he said loudly over the music. "Can I buy you another?"

She looked at his hypnotic smile and tried her best to smile back as she cleared her throat.

"Su-sure," she managed to stammer.

"What are you drinking?" he asked. She could hear a welsh strain in his voice now. Not unusual, seeing as they were in Wales. But, with a nation this small, and the Cardiff University so close, you heard all sorts of accents in clubs like this one.

"Southern Comfort," she said. He gave a little chuckle.

"Fitting," he said.

"Why?" she asked.

"Well, you're American, aren't you?" he asked.

"How'd you guess?" she asked sarcastically. She was used to being asked about her accent. From creepy guys telling her it was hot to people wanting to know where she whether or not it was true that everyone owned a gun in the states, brits seemed fascinated with her nation of origin.

"I guess I have an ear for that kind of thing," he said dryly. Then, he turned towards the bar and signaled the bartender over. As he ordered her another drink, Alana couldn't help but stare at him a little longer.

He was tall. At least a few inches above the rest of the men at the club. His shocking red hair and nicely toned body did indeed make him stand out. And, as she watched him from the bar, Alana caught a very nice view from behind. That was more than impressive as well.

She suddenly felt slightly flushed again as a sensation washed over her that she hadn't experienced in a long time.

The bartender slid the drink across the bar to the red head and he caught it deftly. He turned to Alana and gave her a smile that caused her to melt from the inside out like the chocolate in the middle of a s'more.

She swallowed and tried her best to smile back at him in the cool confident way she'd seen other girls at the bar smile at men. In the end, she was afraid the look came off a bit pathetic. If it did, the redhead didn't seem phased.
"So," he said. "How does a nice American girl like you end up in a dingy club in Wales?"

"Really?" she couldn't help but ask. "That's your line?"

"Who said anything about a line?" he asked. "Maybe I really want to know."

"That's why guys buy girls drinks, right?" she asked. "Because you want to get to know them?"

Maybe she was being too defensive. But, some horrible part in the back of her mind kept waiting for some sort of catch. Guys as good looking as this one simply didn't hit on her. She found herself at an almost complete loss for how to behave and, when that happened, defensiveness became her default position.
The redhead once again impressed her by laughing instead of becoming defensive right back.

"Ok," he said, a note of amusement still lining his voice. "You caught me.

And, since my line didn't work. How about we start with names? I'm Llewelyn. You can call me Lew."

"Alana," she said simply.

"Alana," he echoed with another smile that caused a melty sensation to rush through her stomach. "Nice to meet you."

With what she hoped was a secretive smile, she turned away slightly and sipped at the drink he had given her. Admittedly, as this was her second, her head was starting to feel pleasantly dizzy.

"Now that we've got introductions out of the way," he said. "Maybe you'll be a little more receptive to my question."

"The one about how I ended up here?" she asked. "It's not very interesting."

"I doubt that," he said.

"I'm studying at the university in Cardiff," she said. "Some of the girls in my dorm were coming here tonight and I decided to tag along."

Apparently her attempt to hide the regret in her voice had failed. Because his smile dimmed slightly and he scooted a little closer to her.

"I take it this wasn't your first choice to spend the evening," he said.

"I thought it would be good to actually get out," Alana said. "Turns out I'd rather be back in my room re-reading Fellowship of the Ring."

"I'll try not to take that personally," he said.

"Don't," she told him. "It's not you. I'm just not very social."

"To tell the truth, I'm not either," he said. "This whole thing was my brother's idea."

Lew nodded his head towards the small, brown-haired guy across the bar who was engaged in another unsuccessful pickup attempt. This time, it was an elegant looking girl with long dark hair and a permanent pout on her lips.

"I wouldn't say no to being curled up in my bed reading some Tolkien right now either," he said.

Alana tried to ignore the flush that rushed through her at the thought of this man in bed. Instead, she tried to focus on the second part of his comment. Though, trying to focus on anything was becoming increasingly difficult. Her head was feeling fuzzier by the minute and the world around her had become slightly blurred.

"I wouldn't have taken you for a Tolkien fan," she said, trying to force the increasingly fuzzy sensation away.

"Never judge a book by its cover," he quipped.

They continued to talk about the Tolkien trilogy as well as several other fantasy books that Alana had lately been taken with. She was surprised to learn that Lew had read quite a few of them and the ones he hadn't he seemed very interested in learning about. Alana was half convinced that she was falling in love.

Still, she could not be sure if that was because of Llewelyn or the falling sensation she was beginning to experience as a result of the alcohol.

Though, really, she was certain she had never felt quite this unstable after two drinks.

By the time Lew's brother made his way over to them, Alana was fighting to keep herself standing straight up. She was just cognizant enough to catch a the words Lew and his brother were speaking to each other.

"What are you doing?" Lew's brother asked gesturing fiercely to Alana.

"What does it look like I'm doing?" Lew said in an undertone.

"Just...please tell me you didn't mark her," the brother said, sounding exasperated. Alana squinted as she tried to move towards the brothers. She was now positive that what she was feeling wasn't normal drunkenness. And she needed to know exactly what "marked" meant.

"What-what did you...?" she felt her legs collapse

beneath her as she grabbed a hold of Lew's arm for support. He turned to her and stared directly into her eyes.

"Alana, just keep focused on me," he said urgently. "Everything will be all right. I promise."

Alana could do little but what she was told. She kept her eyes focused completely on his. As she did, his green eyes shined down at her and, through a dizzy haze, she was sure she saw something different, something intriguing in them.

The longer she stared the more they seemed to flash, almost to move. Like the scales of a great animal.

Those strange, moving eyes were the last things she saw before the world around her faded from view.

Chapter Two

"An arferol! He brought an arferol to our Cartref!"

Alana could hear voices above her. Her head was laying on something soft. A pillow. And she felt sheets curled around her body. Clearly, she had been taken somewhere.

The voice that had spoken was one she recognized, but only dimly. The next voice was much more familiar.

"The texts didn't specify that the girl needed to be a Draig," said. "Nor did father before he died. All he said was that we needed to find a girl. Two if possible. And, now, we've found one."

Alana kept her eyes pressed closed hoping that, while they thought she was unconscious, they would explain exactly what they intended to do with her. She'd been kidnapped, that was clear. But, she still had no idea why. And, what's more, she had no idea what these strange words they were using meant.

She thought the words, Arferol, Cartref, sounded welsh. She'd become fairly familiar with the language after six months studying there. At the very least, she knew it when she heard it spoken. But, she'd no idea what they meant. Or what they had to do with her.

"Regardless," a new female voice said. "Now that the girl is here, she can not be allowed to leave. If she did, we would risk exposure or worse." This voice was deep, clear and authoritative. Clearly, the woman was the leader here.

The first voice, which Alana realized belonged to Lew's brother, cursed to the room.

"All is not lost, Owain," the woman said. "We've needed a consort for the men in the clan for years. There are few women now. Those eligible have already been mated. Our young men need someone to express their...urges with. An Arefol girl will do."

Alana felt her blood freeze. Though she still had no idea what Arefol meant or what the clan was, it was now clear what they meant to do with her. They wanted to make her a sex slave. A sex slave for some...weird...cult.

She fought, desperately against the urge to open her eyes, jump from the bed and try to rush out of...wherever she was. She realized that she would need to get out of this. And, if she was going to, she would need to find out everything she could. About who these people were, where she was and what exactly they were planning to do.

"That's not the only option," Lew said firmly.

"We know your theory, Lew," Owain cut in. "Don't-"

"Let your brother speak, Owain," the woman said fiercely. "Remember, now that your father has passed, Lewellyn will become the clan leader."

Even with her eyes closed, Alana could sense the tension in the silence that passed between the three people above her.

"Yes mother," Owain said finally. Though, there was a definite bitter note to his voice.

"The girl is a virgin, I'm sure of it," Lew said. Alana felt the blood rush towards her face and prayed that her blush wasn't noticeable. How he had known about her sexual inexperience was quite beyond her.

"The texts say that a leader may choose a virgin girl for his mate. It does not specify whether that girl should be a Draig or an Arefol."

"No one in the clan has ever been mated to an Arefol," Owain said. "It would be near to blasphemy for a leader to do so."

"Why?" Lew asked fiercely. "The texts don't say-"

"Think about it, Lew!" Owain said. "Children born from an Arefol and a Draig union might not even survive. And if they do, no one knows what abilities they will have if any at all."

"So the option is to continue marrying within the clan?" Lew asked. "Keep on marrying cousins until our people die out entirely? We already have a shortage of women. New blood is needed-"

"Not new Arefol blood!" Owain insisted.

"Enough!" Their mother insisted. The boys stopped their bickering immediately.

"There are still four weeks until Llewelyn's coronation.

We will keep the girl here until then. On the day of the full moon, he will decide what is best to do."

"But mother-" Owain began.

"He will be the clan leader," the Mother said. "It is his decision. I only hope you consider it carefully, Llewelyn. There is too much at stake for our family to gamble our future because of your passion for a pretty arefol girl."

There was a brief silence. Not quite as tense as the one that preceded it but still pregnant with meaning.

"Of course, mother," Llewellyn said.

"That is settled then," the mother said. "Owain and I will leave you now."

Alana listened to the footsteps as the mother and Owain walked away from her bed. A telltale click of the door told her that they had left the room.

Now that they were gone, Alana took a chance and opened her eyes. When she did, she saw those green eyes staring back at her. They looked every bit as fiery and alive as they had in the club. Just before she had fallen to the sticky floor.

"Where am I?" Alana asked.

"Safe. That's all you need to know," he said. "For now."

"Why did you bring me here?" she asked.

"It's complicated," he told her. "And you're in no state to understand it now."

"Yeah," Alana answered fiercely. "I guess being slipped a date rape drug will do that to you."

Now, as the fear was dissipating, a swell of anger began to rise up to her chest and mingle with the anxiety filled beats of her heart.

"I'm sorry I had to trick you," he said. Though he sounded genuine, Alana forced herself not to be moved. Her arms remained folded across her chest and her eyes focused on him glaring darkly.

"Believe me, I wouldn't have if there was any other way," he said.

"Another way to do what, exactly?" Alana asked. She kept the fierceness in her voice as she took stock of the room she was in. It was gigantic by any standards. More of an apartment than a bedroom. She could see a canopy above her bed, a closet to her right. There was a comfortable looking couch just underneath a tall, large window. And, just to the side of that, looked like her only means of escape. A door.

"As I said," Lew told her. "I'll explain it to you as soon as I can. For now, you must stay in this room."

"Like hell!" She said. "You can't make me stay here. People will notice if I disappear-"

"We both know that's not true," Llewellyn said. Alana

felt her face go pale. She wanted to ask how he knew. How he could tell that she was bluffing. But, she had a feeling he knew the same way he had discovered she was a virgin.

Clearly, he knew about her past. He knew that her parents had been killed in a car wreck five years ago. Knew that the aunt and uncle she'd gone to live with in London had little time for her. Knew that she had yet to make any friends at her university.

He was right. No one would notice or care if she disappeared from the face of the earth.

She let that depressing thought sink in before straightening herself up and trying another tactic.

"Will you at least tell me why I won't be allowed out of this room?" she asked folding her arms across her chest. Lewellyn heaved another sigh and put his hand on the bedpost as he turned back to her.

"For now, suffice it to say, there are...people here who will not be so kind to you if you step out alone."

He looked at her with an expression that was well beyond serious. When his eyes looked into hers, it was as though her staying here, in this room was a matter of life and death. The expression forced the fear back into Alana's limbs and she felt her heart begin to pound in a fierce and quick rhythm.

"What sort of people?" she asked quietly.

"You'll see, eventually," he answered. "For now, please

get some rest."

She stared at him a long while, her arms still crossed before deciding that now, when she was alone with Lew, was her best chance to get out of the room. To see what was really going on.

"And what if I want to see now?" she asked.

Before he could say anything more, she stood from the bed and marched purposefully towards the door. She had barely made it two feet before a soft, yet firm hand grabbed hold of her wrist and pulled her back.

When she looked back at Lewellyn, his eyes were desperate, almost fearful. That caused her heart to beat even more quickly.

"Alana, please," he said. "You must promise me you will never go out there alone."

"What will happen if I do?" she asked quietly.

"Just promise me."

Both his hands were clutched over hers now and the pleading expression on his face was more than palpable.

"Fine," she said reluctantly. "I promise."

"Good," he answered breathing a sigh of relief. He led her back to the bed and laid her down underneath the sheets. When he moved the blankets around her, she realized that this was the first time in a long time anyone had tucked her in.

When his warm hand brushed against her shoulder, a sharp, pleasant shiver ran through her body. That had certainly never happened when her parents used to put her to bed.

"Breakfast will be brought up to you in the morning," he said. "As well as some new clothes."

She looked up at him and tried to speak, but, no words seemed able to form in her mouth. She nodded her understanding instead. She was almost glad to see his expression soften when she did.

Alana held her breath as Lewellyn leaned over her, bent down and placed a gentle, lingering kiss on her forehead.

"Goodnight, Alana," he whispered, pulling back.
She tried to say good night as well, tried to express some sort of acknowledgment. But, when she looked into his green eyes, she found that, once again, words failed her. Instead, she nodded once more.

He backed away from the bed, keeping his eyes fixed on her until he reached the door of the room and turned out the light.

As Alana turned to sleep, she found that the last thoughts she had were of Llewellyn and the kiss that still seared on her forehead like a brand.

Chapter Three

When she woke that morning, as promised, breakfast stood ready for her by her bedside. Two eggs over easy, sausage, baked beans a fried tomato and toast along with coffee. It was a much larger meal than she had ever dared to eat in the morning before. But, she got the feeling that these people, whoever they were, were very traditional. And this was what they called a traditional full welsh breakfast.

As she put her feet on the floor and made to grasp for a slice of toast, a small piece of paper caught her eye. She grasped it and unfolded it to find a note in neat, cursive handwriting.

Alana, it began.
I hope you are feeling better this morning. There are fresh clothes for you in the wardrobe. The loo is in the room just to the right side of the bed. There's a shower and bath in there so that you can get cleaned up. Also, I've had them place a small gift for you on the bookshelves beside the window. Think of it as my way of saying "sorry". I expect I'll see you soon.
-Lew

With the note read, Alana still tried as hard as she could to be angry with him. How could she not be angry with a man who had slipped her a roofie and kidnapped her? But, when she looked down at this delicious smelling breakfast and thought of the trouble he had obviously gone to have clothes placed for her and even a gift, it was becoming more and more difficult to stay mad.

The gift piqued her curiosity more than anything else.

Setting her toast down and her feet on the floor, she padded her way over to the bookshelf. There, she could not help the smile that crossed her face.

The large structure, with four shelves full of antique, beautifully bound books, seemed to contain every volume she had mentioned to Lewellyn the night before. Tolkien's entire library was there as well as C.S. Lewis, JK Rowling, Neil Gaiman and a few others that she did not know but sounded promising.

She dressed and washed as quickly as she could. The clothing was just as impressive as the books had been, though less interesting to Alana. Dresses of varying lengths, made of fine silk and beautiful linens hung in her wardrobe. She picked out the simplest of these, a pale blue sundress.

Once she was dressed, she rushed over to the books and immediately selected one of the newer ones which she was anxious to read. She settled herself on the window seat and, looking out, was immediately distracted by a beautiful, ruined stone castle.

The tower was still intact and stood with its pure white stones gleaming against the morning sun. the rest of the structure was moss colored and faded by time. It looked very much like the sort of thing one might come across in a fantasy novel and Alana found herself anxious to explore it.
But, then she remembered Lewellyn's warning.

The pleading look that had laced his eyes the night before. She knew that, whatever was out there, it frightened him. And, if a man as tough as Lewellyn seemed to be was frightened, there was most likely, good reason for it.

So, she tried her best to ignore the castle in favor of her books. It wasn't until just before noon that movement from the ground below caught her eye. She looked down to see that a small group of young men were making their way towards the ruined castle. And, what's more, the young men were shirtless.

Alana gave into her base urge and set the book she was reading aside, deciding instead, to watch these fit young men.

All of them were muscular. Some were well-tanned others were paler. They all seemed to share a matching red tattoo emblazoned across their backs. From a distance, it looked like some sort of great snake.

Some had fair hair some had dark. There was only one head of shocking red hair in the group. That belonged to Lewellyn. His torso was one of the ones that were fairer than the others. Still, the gleam of sunlight on his muscular frame caused a tingling sensation to rush through Alana's chest and straight down to her core.

She watched as the men gathered in a circle. Apparently, performing some sort of ritual. She could barely make out Lewellyn beginning to speak to the group. She wished desperately that she could hear the words being said.

That was when an idea hit her. She could hear the words. After all, Lewellyn had not forbidden her from leaving the room entirely, just from leaving the room alone. The castle was mere feet from the side of the house where her bedroom sat and, once she reached the castle, she would not be alone at all. Lewellyn would be there.

Her mind made up, she opened the bedroom door and rushed down the stairs just to the right of it. When she reached the outside door, she pulled it open as quietly as she could and made her way outside.

The sound of chanting filled the air as Alana found a shrub near the castle large enough to hide behind. From there, she could see the men through the ruined stone as they chanted their strange melody.

It was Welsh, she knew that much, though she could not make out the words. The melody felt ancient, as though it might have been created centuries before.

Suddenly, the voices stopped completely. She watched as each of the men closed his eyes in turn. They grasped hands and, in unison, let out a great yell that echoed along the green cliffs of the landscape.

Alana screamed and shot backward as the men before her each disappeared to be replaced by large, red dragons.

The creatures, apparently oblivious to her, took the sky and began to soar gracefully above the ruined castle and cliffs and trees.

Alana's feet were like lead. Heavy and frozen to the spot where she stood. She could feel her heart thumping inside her chest as though it might explode. She kept her eyes on the dragons circling above the castle and gasped again as one took a beautiful and smooth dive off the cliff on which the house and castle stood.

Without being aware of moving her feet, Alana stepped out of the bushes and made to move towards the place where the diving dragon had disappeared.

As soon as she did, another dragon out of the corner of her eye caught her attention. When she turned towards it, she realized it was flying straight towards her. It's face set in apparent malevolence, smoke rising menacingly from its nostrils.

There was no question now. The creature had seen her.

Chapter Four

With another scream, Alana threw herself to the ground. She barely felt the rock on which she had landed hit and cut her cheek before she streamed again.

Huge talons were closing in on her, moving over her like a cat catching a mouse beneath its paw.

Her stomach gave a strange flip as she felt herself being lifted fully from the ground. She was being carried. She felt the dragon's large tallon beneath her, cutting into her back as he seemed to grasp her fully in his claws.
She looked down as they passed over the large, country manor where she now lived and soared to a spot near the back of the house. Away from the castle and away from the other creatures.

Alana's first instinct as she lay there in this animal's grasp was to call for help. But, she had no voice to do so. And, besides, there was no one to hear her but the other dragons she had seen.

As the beast carrying her began to slow his flight, she noticed that they were reaching the ground. When they hit the grass behind the manner with a large thump, Alanna gave a gasp of surprised as she was released from her hold and tumbled down onto the grass below.

The creature turned away from her and moved to a spot just a few feet left. She watched as it closed its eyes and slowly, began to shift. A minute later, she saw Lewellyn standing before her breathing heavily as though he had just run a great distance and clutching his side.

Alana stood, staring at him, unsure of what to say. Still unsure that she would be able to say anything at all, even if she tried.

Finally, he looked up at her. He gave her a dark glare which she had never seen from him and marched towards her, his face set. For the first time, she was afraid of him.

He grabbed her none too gently by the wrist and pulled her into the back door of the house. Once inside, they moved to the stairwell before he grasped her shoulders and pushed her roughly against the wall.

"What the hell did you think you were doing?" he asked fiercely. Lewellyn could feel his heart pounding. He was not sure if it was anger, fear for Alana, the pain of the shift or a strange combination of all three.

"What-what was that? What are-"

"You realize you could have died," Lew said. Ignoring Alana's shocked stammers "If anyone but me had seen you first, you would have been killed within two minutes or worse."

"How can you...you can shift," Alana said finally. Sounding oddly triumphant though still more than a bit breathless, "I...I mean you can change into-"

"Into a dragon, yes," Lewellyn said reluctantly with more than a trace of annoyance lining his voice.

"When were you planning on telling me that?" Alana

demanded.

"When you were ready," Lew said. "You weren't yet. You should have waited."

"If you had told me the truth from the beginning, I wouldn't have had to," she said as firmly as could, though her voice still shook more than a bit.

He took his hands from her shoulders and ran one hand over his face, looking around the abandoned stairwell as though hoping someone might appear and tell him what to do next. Truth be told, he wished his father were here to give him the advice he so desperately needed. But, he knew that, with his father gone, he would have to make these decisions for himself.

"Are you going to tell me the whole truth now?" Alana asked. When Lewellyn turned back to her, he saw her face set with a hard glare. Those hazel eyes, usually so wide and innocent were now laced with a firm set resolve. She, clearly would not accept anything but the whole truth from him now.

"Yes," he said finally, reluctantly. Alana felt her eyes widen in surprise. She had expected him to put up another fight.

"But not here," he said. He lifted a hand to her cheek. She winced when his thumb ran over a small cut that a jagged rock had given her when she had first pushed herself to the ground.

"I'll need to take a look at that cut," he said. "We'll go back up to your room. I'll explain everything there."

Alana allowed herself to be led up the dark, winding stairwell, back into her large bedroom. Lew opened the door and placed a hand on the small of her back to guide her inside. She shivered at the warmth of his touch through the thin fabric of her summer dress.

For his part, Lew felt no small amount of blood surge through him at even the smallest touch of this young arefol girl. He was certain no draig had ever inspired such a feeling in him as Alana did. In fact, he was certain no woman draig or not had caused his body to respond this way.

He'd felt it first when he'd seen her at the bar. He remembered the moment vividly. Her long dark hair falling into her dark eyes, the tantalizing v neck top she wore that displayed a hint of creamy cleavage. Even the slightly lost expression she had worn that night, as though she was out of her element and looking for a path back home, called out to the beast in him more than anything else he could remember.

And now, as he sat her down on the windowseat, the light from the sun shining on her hair, the pale blue sun dress making her pale skin glow as though begging to be touched, he knew that this girl was dangerous. He could not take her, he realized that. But, oh, how he wanted to.

Instead of acting on this urge, he found a small rag from one of the cupboards, dabbed it with rubbing alcohol and touched it to her cheek.

"This will sting," he warned.

Alana let out a small gasp of pain when the liquid touched her skin but gritted her teeth against it until he removed the cloth for a moment.

"Are you going to tell me?" she asked as firmly as she could when he was so close to her. His breath almost tickling her cheek as he applied his medicine.

Her heart nearly fell in disappointment when he sat back and heaved a sigh. Slowly, he began his story.

Llewellyn told Alana that the dragons of wales were not a myth but, rather, an ancient clan in the region. They were hunted to near extinction in the early Roman centuries and, since, had committed themselves to living in secrecy.

"So, there are more of you?" Alana asked.

"Yes," Llewellyn said. "But, not many now. There are two more small villages of Draig's near Snowdonia. And there's a small community in Cardiff. That is why my brother and I went there last night. We were...searching for girls who might help us."

"Is that why you brought me here?"

Reluctantly, Llewellyn nodded. He knew he could not tell Alana the whole truth. Not yet. She had seen too much that day.

"Our clan is dying out," he explained. "Because we live in secret, we've been intermarrying for years. It's not sustainable. Now, there are very few women left in the clan. The ones who are with us are mated all ready. When my father, the clan leader died, he asked me and my brother to go to Cardiff in order to find a..a girl who could help us."

"How, exactly, was a girl supposed to help?" Alana asked suspiciously. She remembered Lew's brother, Owain, getting upset with Lew for bringing Alana. She remembered that it was because she was an "Arefol". Given this information, she took that to mean simply a 'nonshifter'.

"There's a ritual," Lewellyn said hesitantly. "It takes place at the full moon. A virgin is needed to perform it."

"What happens at this...ritual?" Alana asked nervously.

Lewellyn looked at her wide eyes and felt a stab of guilt when he realized they were filled with fear. He knew he needed to reassure her. Even if the platitudes he offered proved untrue.

"Nothing you should be frightened of," he said finally. "Anyway, it's four weeks until then. You shouldn't worry about it now."

He placed the alcohol laden rag on her cheek once more. This time, she didn't wince. Instead, she looked into his eyes, half hoping and half dreading what she had seen there the night before. The flashing moving creature behind them. The beast behind the man.

Now, there was none of that. There was no beast, no animal; nothing but a man looking back at her, tending to her cut with more tenderness than she had felt from any man before.

"I suppose I should thank you," she said quietly. He stopped running the cloth over her still bleeding cut and looked directly at her. "After all, you did save my life."

She gave him a small shy smile and Lewellyn could see a hint of color enter the girl's cheek. At that look, that one innocent look, he felt his restraint crumble.

"I would do it again," he said quietly.

Then, without thinking, without waiting for his better judgment to protest, he put his hand against her cheek, leaned forward and kissed her.

It was soft, gentle, almost unsure at first. But, as Alana began to open to him, when she pressed back against him, Lew felt his restraint break apart completely.

Soon, his hands were nestled in her long black hair as he pressed her back passionately against the window. When she pressed herself into him, he let out a guttural groan as he felt his member begin to swell.

Finally, after what seemed like ages but, was truly less than a day, he was touching her. Kissing her, feeling her long, soft hair beneath his fingertips.
She let out a sweet, little sound in the back of her throat as Lewellyn felt a tiny hand move to run down his naked torso. More blood drained from his head to his groin as she caressed him. She wrapped her arms around him pulling him more tightly to her.

It was only when one small, delicate hand moved to undo the gold button on his pants that reality returned to him like a splash of ice-cold water. This girl could not be his mate. Not yet.

Reluctantly, he removed one hand from her hair and took the hand that was slowly undoing his trouser button by the wrist. Stopping it's movement.

"We can't," he said quietly.

"Why not?" she asked. Her hazel eyes looked at him and he could see a mixture of confusion, passion and a hint of hurt line her expression.

"I'll explain when I can," he said quickly standing up. "I'll be back in an hour to bring you your lunch."

With that, he hurried from the room leaving Alana, confused and still aroused, staring after him.

The Dragon's Secret:

The Clan Book 2

By:Lea Larsen

© 2016

Table of Contents

Chapter One   37

Chapter Two   45

Chapter Three   50

Chapter Four   62

© **Copyright 2016 by: Lea Larsen All rights reserved.**

This document is geared toward providing exact and reliable information in regard to the topic and issue covered. The publication is sold with the idea that the publisher is not required to render accounting, officially permitted, or otherwise, qualified services. If advice is necessary, legal or professional, a practiced individual in the profession should be ordered.

From a Declaration of Principles which was accepted and approved equally by a Committee of the American Bar Association and a Committee of Publishers and Associations.

In no way is it legal to reproduce, duplicate, or transmit any part of this document in either electronic means or in printed format. Recording of this publication is strictly prohibited and any storage of this document is not allowed unless with written permission from the publisher. All rights reserved.

The information provided herein is stated to be truthful and consistent, in that any liability, in terms of inattention or otherwise, by any usage or abuse of any policies, processes, or directions contained within is the solitary and utter responsibility of the recipient reader. Under no circumstances will any legal responsibility or blame be held against the publisher for any reparation, damages, or monetary loss due to the information herein, either directly or indirectly.

Respective authors own all copyrights not held by the publisher.

The information herein is offered for informational purposes solely, and is universal as so.

The presentation of the information is without contract or any type of guarantee assurance.

The trademarks that are used are without any consent, and the publication of the trademark is without permission or backing by the trademark owner. All trademarks and brands within this book are for clarifying purposes only and are the owned by the owners themselves, not affiliated with this document.

Chapter One

Alana was getting more than a little sick of this life of luxury. She had been stuck in the room where Llewellyn had placed her for nearly three weeks. In that time, the only other soul she had encountered (not counting her foray into the circle of dragons on her first day at the manor) was Llewellyn.

An unseen someone always came into the room before she woke in the morning to provide her with breakfast, new clothes and clean towels for her bath or shower. The dresses they provided her were always lovely, silk things or cute cocktail dresses. They were all beautiful and, she had to admit, looked stunning on her. But after a week of lounging around in silk gowns, she was beginning to miss sweatpants and t-shirts.

Llewellyn came to give her lunch and dinner.

It wasn't that Alana minded seeing Llewellyn. In fact, his visits had become the highlight of her day.

Much to her chagrin, he had not kissed her or even truly touched her again since that first day. In fact, he seemed to be avoiding getting too close to her at all.

They talked, but he always made sure to keep a safe distance. Instead of sitting next to her on the window seat, he would pull a chair out from beside the bed. When he said good night, he made sure to stand a good two feet from her. And, since that very first night, she had felt nothing from him like the searing kiss he had placed on her forehead.

She still yearned to touch him of course, to have him touch her. Every time he gave her that half smile that made him look undeniably sexy. Every time he so much as stretched his hand to reach for his glass so that she could see his well-defined muscles in the too tight t-shirts he wore, it was all she could do not to cross the room and pounce on him.

And, what's more, she had a feeling he felt the same way about her. She'd seen him look her way when they spoke. She had seen the hungry glance he gave her when she leaned over to speak to him. She saw him, barely, almost imperceptibly lick his lips when she stretched in her seat drawing attention to the way the dresses he'd given her clung to the curves of her body.

What she still couldn't figure out was why, if he wanted this as badly as she did—and he clearly did— he was still pushing her away.

She had a feeling that whatever it was had something to do with this ritual he had mentioned. She still hadn't gotten him to tell her anything more about what might actually happen at this ceremony. Nor was he particularly keen to talk about his full moon coronation.

Luckily for Alana, he was more than happy to talk about the rest of his life as a Draig — which, she had learned was the word they used for dragon shifter. And, this was more fascinating than she could have imagined.

"So, I guess you're sort of…born with the ability to do what you do?" she asked one day as Llewellyn sat down for lunch.

She was sitting beside the window, absently chewing on a cream cheese and cucumber sandwich from the tray he had brought for her. He, as usual, was sitting in a high-backed and uncomfortable looking chair a good distance away from her.

"That's right," he said. "It's not something you learn. It's...something you are."

"But, how do they know if you have it when you're born?" she asked.

"The short answer is, they don't," he said. "Though, a child to a mated Draig couple is hardly ever born without the ability to shift. But, it doesn't show itself until a few years later."

"How old were you when you started?" she asked curiously.

"I was three," he answered. "It came on me all of a sudden. I remember feeling terrified."

"Why?" she asked. "Didn't you sort of...decide to do it?"

He shook his head with a slight chuckle.
"It doesn't quite work like that," he said. "See, when we're children, we can't control it. The change just comes upon us when we're scared or particularly angry."

"Which one were you?" she asked.

He set the sandwich he'd been munching down on the tray and looked at her thoughtfully.

"I suppose I was scared," he said. "I don't remember much. I was alone in my bed, it was raining outside. Suddenly, I heard this explosive crack of thunder. The next thing I knew, I was flying above my bed, my nose was long and red and there were little flames shooting from it."

"It's a wonder you didn't burn the house down," Alana said.

"They were too small to cause any real damage then," he answered with a dismissive wave of his hand. "I was lucky that my father came in soon after and was able to calm me down. But, after that, I wasn't allowed to leave the house for years. Not until I took lessons on control from my father and proved to my parents that I could master it."

"I know how your young self must have felt," she said. There was a hint of bitterness in her voice which even she could hear. She made no attempt to hide it.

"Stuck in your house. Not really knowing why. Not knowing when you'll be allowed to leave."

Her eyes glanced absently down to the ruined castle. She knew the sight almost by heart now. The bright stones shimmering in the sunlight, the tower with a doorway and who knows what inside. But, she had long since given up the hope of exploring the structure.

When she turned back, Llewellyn was gazing at her steadfastly.

She wondered if she might have finally convinced him of something. Though she wasn't sure what.

What she had convinced him of was the need for her to leave the room. At least for the evening. Llewellyn knew that she was right. That longing, wistful expression on her face as she glanced out her window was one that he was all too familiar with. He couldn't stand to see her look like that.

"Alana," he began hesitantly. "How would you like to go out tonight?"

"Go where?" Alana asked, her voice mixed with hope and skepticism.

"Out to the castle," he said gesturing to the window. He felt his heart lift when a bright, beaming smile crawled across her face.

"Are you sure?" she asked.

"Of course, I know you want to see it."

For her part, Alana felt her pulse jump in her chest, her heart pound in excitement. After three weeks of nothing but reading and trying on clothes; three weeks of staring longingly at the ruined castle, she was finally going to be able to see it. Perhaps she could even go into the tower. Maybe she could climb its heights and stand at the top looking over at the cliffs and rivers on either side of them.

Maybe, Llewellyn would climb it with her. That thought made her heart pound even quicker.

"Yes!" she said. "I'd love to go out tonight."
"Wonderful," he said. "We'll leave just after dinner."

With that, he said goodbye and left the room. As Llewellyn walked down the stairwell, however, he could not help but worry. Being alone with Alana in a room he could control was one thing.

Her suite had plenty of space and plenty of furniture. He could keep his distance in there.

But, walking with her in the castle, guiding her around the ancient rocks, holding her hand to help her up the rickety stairway in the tower, was going to be another thing entirely.

Breathing a sigh, he leaned back against a wall in the stairwell and prayed to whoever might be listening that he would be able to get through this night with his heart intact.

Chapter Two

The evening came much more quickly than Llewellyn had expected. He'd had a tray sent up to Alana's room with dinner. Usually, he brought it himself but, tonight, he thought it might be best that he not spend more time alone with her than was absolutely necessary.

As it was, he walked out of his own room that evening and towards the stairwell that led to hers with more than a hint of trepidation. As he turned the corner to the stairwell, he was stopped in his tracks by a figure lurking in the shadow of the setting sun.

"I thought the Arefol's dinner had already been sent up."

"Owain," Llewellyn said, breathing a slight sigh of relief at the sight of his brother. "You shouldn't jump out at me like that."

"And you shouldn't be spending as much time as you are with that girl," Owain said moving towards his brother menacingly. Though Owain was not tall or as muscular as many of the men in the tribe, Llewellyn knew better than to underestimate him. His brother was as shrewd and calculating as anyone he had ever met.

In that way, Owain resembled their father much more closely than Llewellyn feared he ever could. Llew and Owain's father knew how to get what he wanted and he could bend anyone to his will.

Even though Llewellyn was older, it was clear that Owain was more his father's son. A fact Owain pointed out frequently. A fact that also made the younger brother desire the clan's throne for himself.

His brother's intentions were made more evident by the way Owain moved towards Llew now. Head thrown back, chest puffed out, reaching his full height. Clearly he was making an attempt to challenge Llew's authority.

Well, Llew thought, if his brother wanted to play that game, he would play too. Llewellyn moved towards Owain stretching to his own full height which stood nearly five inches taller than his brother.

"What I choose to do with the girl is none of your concern," Llewellyn said. He looked in his brother's eyes and waited for Owain to back down. To take a step backward, bow his head and shift his eyes to the floor as the younger man always had in their little dominance battles before.

This time, Owain did not step back. He looked Llewellyn square in the eye.

"Our family, our clan is my concern," Owain said. "I will not see you destroy them."

"And what if Alana can save them?" Llewellyn asked.

"I know your theory," Owain said. "You think we need new blood. You think that will help us. It won't. If you mate with this girl, you'll dilute our blood. We will die out more quickly than we are now."

"You can't know that," Llewellyn said.

"I know enough," Owain answered. "This little girl has turned your head. You think that, because you desire her, you should be able to mate her. Never mind what it might mean for the clan. For your family."

He'd grown tired of this game. He had heard all his brother's arguments against taking an Arefol mate before. He didn't care to listen again. Keeping his eyes on his brother, he pushed past him to move up the stairs.

It was only when Llew turned around to ascend the staircase that Owain spoke again.

"I can stop you from mating her."

Llewellyn stopped dead in his tracks when his brother's voice carried up the stairwell. His blood began to run cold as he turned again to face the younger man. When he did, his brother was wearing a superior smirk that Llewellyn knew all too well.

"All the sacred texts say you need a virgin for a mate," Owain said. "What if I were to pay the Arefol a little visit in her room tonight?"

"You wouldn't dare," Llewellyn said. His voice came out as a low growl without his will or approval.

"I would," Owain said. The smile fading from his face. "I would do that and more to save my family. I wonder if you can say the same."

In a flash, Llewellyn launched himself down the stairs. Before he was fully aware of himself, he found that he had pushed his brother against the wall of the hallway. His arms pinning him to the hard surface.

"If you so much as touch her," Llewellyn growled, his face mere inches from Owain's. "I swear, I will kill you. Family or not."

Owain looked back at Llewellyn defiantly for a moment before lowering his head and averting his gaze in submission. As soon as he did, Llewellyn released his hold on his brother and allowed him to walk away.

"Well then," Llewellyn said as he reached the hallway entrance. "I suppose I've got my answer."

Llew saw just a hint of that horrible, superior smirk cross his brother's face before the younger man turned the corner and disappeared.

Chapter Three

Alana paced the space between the window seat and her bed anxiously. She'd already done her make-up, spritzed herself with an assortment of perfumes Llew had set out for her in the restroom and checked her hair twice.

She'd remembered feeling this way on nearly every first date she had ever been on. The fretting, the excited anticipation were all the same. The only difference was, this was not a date. Not really.

The truth was, she wasn't sure what she was to Llew and, what's more, she had no idea what he expected her to be. Sometimes, the way they talked, it was as though they were dating. But, other times, she felt as though they were barely friends.

Somehow, she knew it all hung on this mysterious ritual that he refused to tell her about. Well, she wasn't putting up with that anymore. She was going to get the truth about this "ritual" out of him tonight if it was the last thing she did.

When a knock sounded on her door, she jumped and, with an excited little bounce moved to answer it.

"You look beautiful," Llewellyn said as soon as he caught sight of her. She couldn't help but blush as he took in the red cocktail dress and flat ballet slippers she'd chosen for the occasion.

"I guess it's not great for scaling ancient ruins," she said. "But, then again, nothing in my wardrobe is."

She realized too late that he might take that as an insult to his taste in clothing. After all, she supposed it was Llewellyn who was picking out her beautiful wardrobe. The last thing she wanted to do was make him think she was ungrateful.

Luckily for Alana, Llewellyn did not think anything of the sort. In fact, he was too taken in by the way the red dress hugged her curves perfectly, stopping just at the knee. The way the skin on her neck gleamed in the light of the setting sun moving through the window. So soft he could almost reach out and touch it.

"You're perfect," he said and meant it. Though, he realized that if he was to avoid the very pitfalls he feared, he should stop staring at her.

"Shall we go?" he asked.

She nodded and he lead her down the stairwell and out through the back door.

Alana had come out this way once before. When she discovered what Llew truly was. Though, on that day, she had been forced to creep outside as quietly as she could. And, her mind had been so filled with men shifting into dragons that there had been very little room for anything else.

Now, this spot seemed different. Greener. Safer, she supposed, now that Llew had grabbed hold of her hand and was guiding her to the ruins of the ancient castle.

"It's so beautiful here," she said.

"I suppose it is," he answered.

"You suppose?"

"I've never been anywhere else," he said with a shrug. "So, I can't really make an informed decision."

"You've never been outside of Wales?" she asked, her eyes narrowing in curiosity. He shook his head 'no'.

"Too dangerous," he said. "Even though I can control my shifting now, there's no telling what might happen alone on the road. When we do travel, we go in pairs or groups. And, it's almost always on some mission for the clan."

"Like the one in Cardiff?" she asked.

He nodded 'yes'. When they stopped at one of the larger stones, he looked out towards the setting sun behind the cliffs in the west. The expression he wore was one of sad desperation. Almost as though he was trapped.

She knew the feeling well. Though, oddly, now that she was here, not in her room, but roaming a ruin with Llewellyn by her side, she didn't feel trapped anymore. In fact, she felt freer than she had ever felt in her life.

Alana closed her eyes and leaned against one of the standing stones that had once made up the castle wall. She listened to the rush of the small creek just down the hill, felt the breeze on her face and thought, for the first time since she had left America, she may have found a place where she could belong.

"Is there anything you wanted to see in particular?" Llewellyn asked, causing her to open her eyes.
"Yes," she answered, suddenly remembering the one thing she had been the most curious about. "Could we climb to the top of the tower."

Llewellyn smiled and offered her his hand as he led her to the ancient stone archway that had once held a door. He led her up the stairs hearing her small footsteps echo against the rocks.

Finally, they reached the top of the tower and looked out to the mountains and cliffs beyond.

The sun had nearly set now, casting the sun in a mixture of orange, yellow, purple and pink hues.

"Wow," she whispered, rushing towards the edge of the tower.

Llewellyn heard her gasp once again as she leaned over and looked down at the valley below them.

"I feel like I can see the world from here," she said.

"We can see a world," he said. "And, that's always been enough for me."

She didn't answer but continued to survey the ground below, finally, her eyes came to rest on a large circle of stones in the middle of the castle ruin. She would have dismissed it as yet another sign of decay if these particular stones had not been placed so deliberately.

"What are those?" she asked pointing to the stones and looking to Llewellyn.

He did not answer right away. He was thinking how best to tell her. He knew he had to at some point. It only made sense to do it here. Now that she was happier and out of the house.

Still, he took a large painful breath before saying.

"That is where the ritual...the coronation will take place next week."

"Ah, is that what this mysterious ritual is? A coronation?" she asked in a teasing voice. The flirty smile she gave him only served to twist his heart more painfully. How could he tell her about the choice she would have to make? How could he tell her what was at stake for his family? His clan?

Well, he supposed, it was best to start at the beginning.

"There's more to it than that," he said. "During this ritual, I will be officially made leader of the clan. And, when I am made leader, I must choose a mate."

"A mate?" she asked. Though she had to admit, she already had a good idea what that might mean.

"A...a wife, I suppose you would call it," he said. "Once the woman I choose and I are mated, we are bound for life. It's a sacred bond that we can not break."

"I see," she said. So, Llewellyn wanted her to be his...wife? It was overwhelming surely. But, she discovered, the idea caused a smile to creep across her face. It caused her heart to flutter more in excitement than anxiety.

"That's not all," he said. "When I choose a mate, we will have to...consummate our relationship in front of the witnesses at the ritual."

"You mean you'll have to have your...wedding night...in front of an audience?" she asked.

"Essentially, yes," he said.

Well, that did make things more complicated. And, as much as she loved talking in hypotheticals, it was about time, she thought that they spoke frankly about her role in all of this.

"And...I guess...that's why you brought me here?" she asked timidly.

"Yes and no," he said sounding reluctant. Her eyes narrowed and a confused frown lined her lips.

"You see because you are...not one of our clan," he said. "My brother and several of the others think you would make a better...consort than a mate."

"Consort?" she asked. Though, she had a feeling that this was what she had heard Llew, his brother, and their mother discuss the night she was brought to the manor.

"You see," he said. "Since we have so few women, the men in our clan need to release their urges. In ages before, we've used non-clan members as consorts to...fulfill those needs."

"So, I would be a prostitute?" she asked. Though she knew that wasn't exactly the term for it. Sex slave would be more accurate.

"If you were to be made a consort," he said. "You would be sterilized so that you could not have children. Then, you would be at the mercy of every man in the clan whenever he wanted you. Day or night."

The horror of that filled her irrevocably. So much so that she looked down at the ground and felt tears beginning to well up in her eyes.

"Alana," Llewellyn said softly. He touched her chin and brought her gaze up to meet his. "Please, know that is not what I want for you."

"Then the only other option," Alana said, swallowing hard and looking into his eyes. "Is to...consummate my relationship with you...in front of potentially hostile witnesses."

"I know it's not ideal," he said. "And, if...if that is not what you want either. If you don't want to be my mate...I suppose I could find a way to sneak you out of the manor. But, you should be warned that the clan will likely find you, no matter where you go, and I can't protect you out there."

She nodded and pulled away from him moving to the edge of the tower again. Her mind spinning. She had dreamed, for weeks of Llew taking her, of him dominating her, making her his.

Now, she had the opportunity. And, what's more, he seemed to want that from her as well. But...it would be her first time. In front of an audience. What if she faltered? What if she wasn't any good at it?

Still, when she thought of the alternatives...they were both too horrible to imagine. Either live life as a slave to dozens of men or leave Llew and the beauty of this place behind forever.

"Alana," Llew said softly, coming up behind her. She let out a sharp breath when he put a gentle hand on her shoulder. "What are you thinking?"

As the last light from the sun faded behind a large mountain to the west, she turned to him, barely making out his face in the darkness.

"I think," she began slowly. "That given the choice of sex slave or sex with a gorgeous man in front of an audience, I'll take the latter."

He looked at her a long moment as though unable to believe what she had just said. Then, slowly, a smile crept over his face.

"Besides," she said, smiling at him in turn. "I don't want to leave here. It's the first place I've really felt at home in, for years."

"Well, I'm glad of that," he said. "Now, it's dark. We should go inside."

He offered her his hand which she gratefully took and he began to lead her down the tower steps and out into the ruin.

As they made their way to the back door, Llewellyn found that he could not keep the smile from his face. She was going to be his mate. This girl. This amazing, beautiful, intelligent young woman was going to be his forever.

Knowing this, it was all he could do not to wrap her in his arms and take her right there, ritual and tradition be damned. Her small hand in his as they climbed the stairs and the sight of her back in that red dress as a long dark braid cascaded down her back did nothing to weaken his desire.

When they reached her room, she turned to him and smiled. "Thank you for tonight," she said. "I needed it."

"I know," he answered. Trying to keep his senses from filling with the scent of her perfume. "I think we both did."

She smiled again and his heart stopped as she reached up on her toes and gave him a soft, lingering kiss on his cheek. The warmth of her lips against his skin, the scent of her perfume, caused him to lose all resolve.

Before he knew what he was doing, he grabbed hold of her shoulders, pushed her into the room and closed the door before pressing his lips desperately against hers.

Alana felt his member press against her leg through the thin fabric of her dress as Llewellyn shoved her against the hard wood of the door.

There was nothing at all soft or gentle about this kiss. His tongue pushed forcefully inside her mouth as though he was trying to invade her very soul. She moaned when she felt one of his hands move up to her breast just as his lips bit and sucked the skin at her neck.

He nibbled at her jawline before bringing his lips up to trace the outside of her ear.

"Do you have any idea what you do to me, Alana?" he asked. "Do you know how long I've wanted to grab you and fuck you until you forget everything else?"

A surge of moisture flooded to her core as she reveled in the feel of his hands running up and down his torso. Suddenly, she knew she wanted to be much more active in this process, as inexperienced as she was, she knew that Llew would teach her.

Hesitantly, she reached her hand to the crotch of his trousers and covered his member.

The low moan he let out gave her a little swell of victory. She reached up behind his neck and gave him a brief kiss before moving her lips to his ear.

"Why don't you show me?" she asked.

With another growl, he pushed her back against the door as her hand continued to stroke the member still growing beneath his trousers.

Llewellyn, moved his own hand underneath her dress to touch her desire through her panties. Even over the fabric he could feel how warm and wet she was.

And it was all for him. She belonged to him.

No, wait. That wasn't right. She would belong to him. But, she did not yet. She couldn't until the ritual. The other members of the clan would know if she was not a virgin when he took her the night of the full moon. They would sense it as he had when he first met her.

If they did, there was no telling what they might do.

Once again, this desperate pleasure was brought to an end by the sobering thought of duty. He took his hand away from her center and grabbed hold of her wrist, prying it from his own member. Still painfully erect inside his pants.

"What is it?" she asked as he pulled away from her.

"I've told you," Llewellyn said. "We can't."

"Why can't we?" she demanded. "Llew...don't you see...I want this! I want to be mated to you!"

That, very nearly, broke his resolve. Hearing those words from her, that she wanted him just as much as he wanted her, were like a thousand aphrodisiacs at once.

She reached up on her toes again and pulled him down for another kiss. It took all the strength he had in him to push her away once again.

"Not yet," he whispered moving closer to her. Gently, he took her face in his hands and placed a searing kiss on her forehead. Just as he had done her first night at the manor.

He backed out of the room with his eyes still locked on her. He didn't take his eyes off her form until he turned to move down the stairwell.

As soon as he was gone, Alana closed the door as loudly as she could in her frustration. She dressed and readied herself for bed hoping against hope that the routine of those actions would chase away thoughts of Llew. Would fend off the arousal still stirring inside of her.

It didn't. Even when she slid into bed, she couldn't help but remember the feeling of his warm lips against her skin. His smooth hands against her bare shoulders, the sound of his voice in her ear. The heat from his skin as he touched her almost where she desperately needed to feel him.

Without thinking, she reached her hand up her nightgown as she retraced the steps Llewellyn's hands had taken not one hour before. When she closed her eyes, she imagined what might have happened if he hadn't stopped.

She imagined him taking those firm fingers and seeking out the very center of her desire. Beneath the covers, eyes still closed, she did just that. She let out a small gasp of pleasure as her fingers found her center and she forced her eyes to remain closed, imagining Llewellyn's hand in place of her own.

She imagined him pressing her hard against the wall of this bedroom and shoving both of his fingers inside her. She let out a small, sharp cry as her own fingers followed the instruction of the image in her mind.

She imagined him replacing his fingers with the long slender cock she had felt beneath his trousers. She imagined him tossing her on the bed and pounding in and out of her so quickly that she barely had time to breathe.

As it was, tension was building inside of her; it was all she could do not to scream out fully into the room. Still, she kept her eyes closed as she imagined the sound of his voice. His warm, sweet breath tickling her ear.

"Come for me, Alana," he said in her mind. "Let me hear you."

"Oh, god! Llew!" she called out into the room.

As she came down from her ecstasy, ragged and spent, she could only pray that no one nearby had heard her embarrassing exclamation.

And, as she turned out her light for bed, she knew that the ritual next week could not come soon enough.

Chapter Four

Sleep brought no relief from thoughts of Llewellyn. He wandered in and out of her dreams like a corporeal spirit. She would feel his hands touching her, his mouth on hers, his breath against her neck.

At one point, the dream became so vivid that she was certain she was not dreaming at all. This was confirmed when she opened her eyes and found herself very much awake in her own room.

Awake, with a man's hand moving slowly down her chest and a large figure looming over her.

"Llew?" she asked hazily to the room.

The figure bent down close enough that his face could be seen in the faint beams of the moonlight.

Dark, unfamiliar eyes shone down on her from inside a face which she barely recognized. It took a moment for her to realize what she was seeing.

The figure was certainly not Llew.

Alana opened her mouth to scream, to call out to the rest of the house but, as soon as she did, this strangely familiar figure put a firm hand against her mouth.

"One scream and I will snap your neck," the dark voice said ominously.

It was only after he spoke that Alana was truly able to place the man before her. This was Owain, Llewellyn's brother.

She saw him smile in the beams of the moonlight which, for some reason, looked brighter than they had been before. She turned her head as much as the hand on her mouth allowed and saw that her window had been thrown open. No doubt that was how the intruder had made his way into her room.

His superior smirk still present, Owain's hand continued his path down the front of her nightdress. When he dipped beneath her clothes, Alana instinctively began to kick and cry out into his hand.

Her cries became sharper when he touched her through her panties.

"I see you've already started," he said in a horrible, condescending voice when he touched the warm wet substance still present in her underwear.

When he forced a hand inside her underwear and reached her folds, Alana gasped and gave an instinctive kick with her leg. It caught him in his shin which caused him to take the hand off her mouth.

"Help!" she screamed instantly as she rolled out from under him and jumped from the bed. "Someone help me!"

"Get back here, Arefol whore," he growled.

She felt her hair being yanked back and screamed full into the room as she was thrown down hard onto the floor. He was on top of her almost immediately, grabbing her night dress and pulling it up over her thighs.

"No one's going to think of mating you after this," he said bringing a hand to his own trousers and beginning to unbutton them.

Another bang sounded from the door of her room. And, in a flash, a larger pair of arms snaked their way around Owain's chest and yanked him away from her.

As Llewellyn pulled his brother to his feet, he saw their mother rush over to Alana whose night dress had been torn in one strategic spot and was now sporting a bruise on her arm.

When the girl looked up at Llewellyn, tears in her eyes and a look of utter shame on her face, he felt something come over him that he had not felt in a long time.

He turned back to his brother and an anger he could not possibly control welled up inside of him.

Alana screamed for the third time that night as the fully formed red dragon began tearing through her bedroom.

"Get down," the woman next to Alana said, "As far as you can." She felt a push as the woman shoved her underneath the bed. As she did, Alana heard the sound of glass breaking and growls and animal's screams.

When she dared to peek out once more, she realized that there were now two dragon's, one slightly smaller than the first, locked in a fearsome battle.

When the largest red one swiped at the smaller dragon's wing, the smaller beast let out a horrible screech of pain. The next moment, the tail of the large dragon flicked so fiercely that it sent her entire bookshelf flying out the open window.

Another fierce tail flick from the large dragon caught the small one directly in the middle, sending him careening backward until he too, fell out the window, screaming and growling until he landed with a thunderous crash.

"No!" the woman beside Alana cried out hysterically.

It was his mother's cry that brought Llewellyn back. He closed his eyes and felt the change slip back over him. As soon as it did, he rushed as quickly as he could over to the window.

When he reached it, his heart stopped cold and he stood still as a statue.

The darkness revealed very little. But, one beam of moonlight, unfortunately placed, told Llew everything he needed to know.

There, amid the dark ivy and night blooming flowers of the manor's garden lay his brother. Dead.

A

The Dragon's Mate: The Clan Book 3

LEA LARSEN

© 2016

© COPYRIGHT 2016 BY: LEA LARSEN ALL RIGHTS RESERVED

ALL RIGHTS RESERVED. NO PART OF THIS BOOK MAY BE USED OR REPRODUCED IN ANY MATTER WHATSOEVER WITHOUT

PERMISSION IN WRITING FROM THE AUTHOR EXCEPT IN THE CASE OF

BRIEF QUOTATIONS EMBODIED IN CRITICAL ARTICLES OR REVIEW.

Chapter one   70

Chapter Two   77

Chapter Three   86

Chapter Four   92

CHAPTER ONE

"THERE CAN BE NO QUESTION OF MATING THE GIRL NOW."

HIS MOTHER PACED BACK AND FORTH IN FRONT OF A LONG, CURTAINED WINDOW IN HER BEDROOM. IT WAS AFTERNOON. NEARLY A WEEK SINCE HIS BROTHER'S DEATH. SINCE THAT TIME, LLEWELLYN HAD SEEN ALANA ONLY ONCE. THE MORNING AFTER, HE WENT UP TO HER ROOM TO MAKE SURE THAT SHE WAS ALL RIGHT. SHE ASSURED HIM THAT SHE WAS.

"DON'T WORRY ABOUT ME," SHE'D SAID. "I CAN TAKE CARE OF MYSELF. YOU NEED TO LOOK AFTER YOUR MOTHER NOW."

IT WAS EASY TO PRETEND THAT WAS WHY HE HAD STAYED AWAY FROM HER ROOM. WHY HE HAD SENT ALL HER MEALS UP WITHOUT BRINGING THEM HIMSELF.

THE TRUTH WAS, HE WAS AFRAID TO FACE HER. AFRAID TO CONFRONT THE NEWS HE KNEW WAS COMING. AFRAID TO FACE WHAT HIS MOTHER WAS FINALLY TELLING HIM NOW.

"I DON'T SEE WHY NOT," LLEWELLYN SAID QUIETLY. HIS MOTHER STOPPED HER FRANTIC PACING AND STARED AT HIM WITH A FIERCE

EXPRESSION IN HER EYES.

"DON'T YOU?" SHE ASKED. "THE DEATH OF A CLAN MEMBER IS NO SMALL THING. THE DEATH OF YOUR BROTHER SHOULD NOT BE TAKEN LIGHTLY. ESPECIALLY NOT BY YOU."
"I DON'T TAKE IT LIGHTLY," LLEWELLYN SAID DEFENSIVELY. "BUT, I STILL SAY THAT OWAIN WAS THE ONLY ONE TO BLAME FOR HIS DEATH. HE WAS THE ONE WHO BROKE INTO ALANA'S ROOM WHEN BOTH YOU AND I HAD FORBIDDEN IT. HE WAS THE ONE WHO TRIED TO…"

HE BROKE OFF, STILL UNABLE TO SAY THE WORD. UNABLE TO CONFRONT WHAT NEARLY HAPPENED TO ALANA, WHAT HIS BROTHER NEARLY PUT HER THROUGH.

"I KNOW," HIS MOTHER SAID MORE QUIETLY. UNDERSTANDING LACING HER VOICE. "BUT THE CLAN WON'T SEE IT THAT WAY."

"IF THE CLAN NEEDS SOMEONE TO BLAME, THEN LET THEM BLAME ME," LLEWELLYN SAID DESPERATELY. "I'M THE ONE WHO DAMAGED OWAIN'S WING. I'M THE ONE WHO PUSHED HIM OUT THE WINDOW. I SHOULD BE PUNISHED FOR HIS DEATH."

"YOU ARE THE CLAN LEADER," HIS MOTHER SAID. "ALANA IS NOTHING MORE THAN AN AREFOL GIRL. THEY WOULD NOT THINK TO PUNISH YOU WHEN THEY SEE HER AS MORE

THAN CULPABLE."

LLEWELLYN STOOD SLOWLY FROM HIS WOODEN CHAIR AND WALKED BEHIND IT. HE CLUTCHED THE BACK OF THE COLD WOOD, LOOKING DETERMINATELY AWAY FROM HIS MOTHER.
HE KNEW SHE WAS RIGHT. THE CLAN WOULD NOT LISTEN TO REASON. THEY WOULD NOT PUNISH THEIR OWN WHEN THERE WAS AREFOL BLOOD READY AND WAITING TO BE SPILLED.

NO, THE ONLY TWO OPTIONS LEFT FOR ALANA WERE DEATH OR A LIFE OF SEXUAL SLAVERY. THE LATTER WOULD BE SEEN AS PUNISHMENT ENOUGH. AND, THE MEN'S URGES WERE DESPERATE ENOUGH TO OVERLOOK THE DEATH OF A CLAN MEMBER.

IF SHE WOULD NOT AGREE TO BECOME A CONSORT FOR THE CLAN, AND LLEWELLYN WAS CONVINCED THAT HE WOULD NEVER, EVER ALLOW HER TO AGREE TO SUCH A PROSPECT, THE ONLY OTHER OPTION WAS DEATH. ON THE NIGHT OF THE FULL MOON, THE MEN OF THE CLAN WOULD EITHER HAVE THEIR LUST OR THEIR BLOOD LUST QUENCHED. THERE WAS NO AVOIDING IT. UNLESS…

"WHAT IF SHE DISAPPEARED BEFORE THE CEREMONY," LLEWELLYN SAID, LOOKING UP FOR THE FIRST TIME AT HIS MOTHER. SHE

LOOKED AT HIM WITH HER MOUTH PURSED CLOSED.

"YOU KNOW THAT'S NOT POSSIBLE," SHE SAID. "THEY WOULD FIND HER."

"NOT IF SHE LEAVES DURING THE RITUAL," HE SAID. "NOT IF SHE'S ALREADY HALFWAY ACROSS THE SEA BY THE TIME IT'S FINISHED."

THIS TIME, HIS MOTHER'S EYES WENT WIDE, HER SKIN TURNED PALE. SHE SEEMED TO REALIZE NOW THAT HE WAS, TRULY SERIOUS ABOUT THIS.

"LLEW YOU...YOU COULDN'T," SHE SAID QUIETLY. "THEY ARE EXPECTING A GIRL. THEY WERE PROMISED AN AREFOL. IF YOU DON'T DELIVER HER…"

"I KNOW WHAT THEY'LL DO," LLEWELLYN SAID. "I'M WILLING TO TAKE THAT CHANCE."

HIS MOTHER STARED AT HIM FIXEDLY, HER EYES HARDENING WITH EACH PASSING MOMENT.

"I SEE," SHE SAID. "AND, I SUPPOSE YOU'RE WILLING TO ALLOW ME TO GO THROUGH THE PAIN OF LOSING BOTH MY SONS IN ONE WEEK?"

LLEWELLYN ONCE AGAIN AVERTED HIS GAZE. THE TRUTH WAS, HE HAD THOUGHT OF that. He remembered his mother's tears after Owain died. They felt worse than her tears after his father's passing. Perhaps because there had been time to prepare when his father passed. But, with Owain…

He could not deny that his mother's cry as his brother fell through that window still haunted him. He knew it always would. All the same, he could not allow Alana to pay the price for it.

"There's no other way, Mom," he said.

"I warned you," she said fiercely. "I warned you not to let your passion for that girl cloud your judgment and that's exactly what it's done."

"Would you rather she die?" Llewellyn asked. "Would you rather I had more blood on my hands?"

"I would rather you put the needs of your family above your own," she said.

Llewellyn opened his mouth to retort but thought better of it. Arguing with his mother would do him no good. He would not change his mind and, he knew that she would not change hers.

"Mother," he said as gently as he could.

"I'M GOING TO GET HER OUT. NO MATTER WHAT YOU SAY. I'M NOT ASKING YOU TO GET INVOLVED. ALL I NEED IS YOUR PROMISE THAT YOU WON'T TELL THE OTHERS."

HER EYES, AS BRIGHT GREEN AS HIS OWN, FLASHED AS HER PALE LIPS REMAINED PURSED IN A FROWN.

"AS THAT WOULD FORCE THEM TO KILL YOU MORE QUICKLY," SHE SAID. "YOU CAN HAVE MY PROMISE THAT I WON'T TELL THEM." LLEWELLYN NODDED AS HIS MOTHER TURNED AWAY FROM HIM AND BACK TO THE WINDOW WHICH LOOKED OUT TO A PLAIN MEADOW, THE SHADOW OF MOUNT SNOWDON IN THE DISTANCE. RECOGNIZING HIS MOTHER'S SIGNAL THAT THEIR CONVERSATION WAS FINISHED, HE TURNED TO THE DOOR AND LEFT THE ROOM.

NOW, ALL THAT WAS LEFT TO DO WAS WHAT ONLY ONE WEEK AGO SEEMED UNTHINKABLE. HE HAD TO SEND ALANA AWAY. AND WITH HER, ANY HOPE EITHER HE OR HIS CLAN HAD OF A FUTURE.

CHAPTER TWO

ALANA STARED OUT THE WINDOW THAT MORNING AS SHE HAD DONE EVERY MORNING SINCE THAT NIGHT.

THOUGH LLEW HAD RESTOCKED HER LITTLE LIBRARY WHICH HAD BEEN DESTROYED, SHE FOUND THAT BOOKS COULD NO LONGER HOLD HER INTEREST. NEITHER, IT SEEMED COULD THE RUINED CASTLE OR THE LARGE GREEN CLIFFS THAT SURROUNDED IT.

WHEN SHE LOOKED OUT OF THE WINDOW NOW, SHE LOOKED DOWN ONTO THE DARK PATCH OF IVY WHERE THE BODY HAD FALLEN NOT ONE WEEK BEFORE. SHE STARED HARD AT THE PATCH AS THOUGH HER GAZE COULD MAKE IT WHAT IT WAS BEFORE. AN ORDINARY PATCH OF IVY AMIDST A DOZEN OTHERS.

PERHAPS IF SHE STARED LONG ENOUGH, IF SHE TRANSFORMED IT IN HER MIND, EVERYTHING ELSE WOULD CHANGE AS WELL. MAYBE SHE WOULDN'T KEEP SEEING OWAIN'S FACE LOOMING ABOVE HER WHEN SHE CLOSED HER EYES. MAYBE SHE WOULDN'T SHUDDER AT THE MEMORY OF HIS UNWELCOME HAND FORCING ITSELF INTO HER.

MAYBE, JUST MAYBE, IF SHE ERASED THE

ENTIRE EVENT FROM HER MIND, LLEWELLYN WOULD COME BACK TO HER. MAYBE HE WOULD TAKE HER IN HIS ARMS AND TELL HER THAT SHE WOULD STILL BE HIS, NO MATTER WHAT ELSE HAD HAPPENED.

SHE HAD NOT SEEN HIM SINCE THE DAY AFTER. HE'D COME TO HER ROOM TO MAKE SURE THAT SHE WAS ALL RIGHT. WHEN SHE ASSURED HIM THAT SHE WAS, HE LEFT. AND THAT WAS THAT.

OF COURSE, SHE TOLD HERSELF, HE'D NEEDED TO TAKE CARE OF HIS MOTHER. SHE'D EVEN TOLD HIM THAT SHOULD BE HIS FIRST PRIORITY. IT WAS ONLY NATURAL THAT HE'D HEEDED HER ADVICE.

BUT NOW, IT WAS THE DAY OF THE CORONATION. AND, SHE STILL HAD NO IDEA WHERE SHE STOOD WITH LLEW. IF HER ROLE HAD CHANGED. AND, IF IT HAD, WHAT THAT ROLE MIGHT BE.

ABSENTLY, SHE RAN HER HAND ALONG THE WINDOWSILL AND LIFTED HER EYES FROM THE PATCH OF IVY. SHE SOUGHT OUT THE LARGE STANDING STONES IN THE MIDDLE OF THE RUINED CASTLE AND THOUGHT OF THE RITUAL.

LLEWELLYN WAS SUPPOSED TO TAKE A MATE TONIGHT. NOW, GIVEN WHAT HAD HAPPENED, SHE HAD NO IDEA IF HE WOULD.

Perhaps the ritual would not happen at all.

Either way, she needed Llewellyn here. If things had changed…if he no longer wanted her…she needed to hear it from him.

Alana jumped in surprise when the door to her room clicked open. She turned and her eyes widened to see Llewellyn striding inside as though her thoughts had summoned him.

He issued no greeting but carried a large brown suitcase and hastily threw it open onto the bed.

"Llew, what—"

"You need to leave," he said.

She felt her heart drop in her chest, the blood draining from her face.

"Leave?" she asked breathlessly.

"This afternoon. You'll sneak down the back stairs into the kitchens at exactly three o'clock. There will be no one there to see you then."

Without looking at her, he hastily moved to her wardrobe and placed a

PILE OF CLOTHES ON THE BED. SHE MOVED SLOWLY TOWARDS HIM.

"BUT...BUT WHAT ABOUT THE CEREMONY?" SHE ASKED.

"DON'T WORRY ABOUT THAT," HE SAID. "I'LL HANDLE IT ON MY OWN. YOU HAVE TO GET OUT."

"YOU...YOU SAID THEY WOULD FIND ME NO MATTER WHERE I WENT," SHE SAID, HOPING THIS ARGUMENT MIGHT STOP HIM IN HIS TRACKS. IT DIDN'T, HE CONTINUED TO RUSH ABOUT THE ROOM, SETTING THINGS ONTO HER BED SO THAT SHE COULD PLACE THEM IN THE LARGE SUITCASE.

"THE CLAN DOESN'T TRAVEL ACROSS THE SEA," HE SAID. "I'VE BOUGHT YOU A ONE-WAY TICKET TO NEW YORK. YOU SHOULD BE SAFE THERE."

SHE LOOKED AT HIM TRYING HER BEST TO THINK OF SOME OTHER ARGUMENT. SOME LOGICAL REASON FOR HER TO REMAIN HERE. THERE WAS NOTHING LEFT FOR HER OUT IN THE REST OF THE WORLD, SHE WAS SURE OF THAT. NO MATTER WHERE SHE WENT NOW, SHE WOULD NEVER BE ABLE TO CALL IT HOME. NOT WITH LLEWELLYN AND THE MANNER AND THE RUINED CASTLE STILL IN HER MIND.

"WHAT IF I SAID NO," SHE TOLD HIM. "WHAT IF I SAID I DON'T WANT TO GO?"

THE FIRM RESOLVE IN HER VOICE MADE HIM STOP BESIDE THE BED. HE PUT BOTH HANDS BESIDE THE SUITCASE AND LOOKED DOWN AT IT AS THOUGH HOPING IT MIGHT PROVIDE SOME COMFORT.

"YOU HAVE TO, ALANA," HE SAID.

"NO, I DON'T," SHE SAID FIRMLY WALKING TOWARDS HIM. "I TOLD YOU I WANT TO BE YOUR MATE. AND I MEANT IT."

SHE TOUCHED HIS ARM GENTLY THEN TOUCHED HIS CHEEK FORCING HIM TO LOOK INTO HER DARK EYES.

HE HAD NOT SEEN THOSE EYES IN NEARLY A WEEK. NOW THAT HE LOOKED INTO THEM, HE REALIZED JUST HOW MUCH HE HAD MISSED HER. HIS HEART LEAPED IN HIS CHEST WHEN SHE PULLED CLOSER TO HIM.

"I DON'T CARE WHAT ANYONE ELSE HAS TO SAY," SHE SAID. "I'M NOT GOING ANYWHERE."

WITH THAT, SHE CLOSED THE GAP BETWEEN THEM AND PUT HER LIPS DESPERATELY ON HIS. IT TOOK ALL THE STRENGTH HE POSSESSED TO PUSH HER AWAY.

"ALANA," HE SAID. "THEY'LL KILL YOU."

HER EYES WIDENED AND HER FACE LOST A BIT OF ITS COLOR AS SHE STEPPED BACK.

"MEMBERS OF THE CLAN BEGAN CALLING FOR YOUR BLOOD AS SOON AS THEY HEARD WHAT HAPPENED," HE TOLD HER. "IF YOU DON'T LEAVE...IF YOU COME TO THIS RITUAL TONIGHT...YOU WON'T COME OUT OF IT ALIVE."

SHE STAYED VERY STILL IN HER SPACE BY THE WINDOW. HE COULD SEE RED FORMING AT THE CORNERS OF HER EYES, WATER POOLED INSIDE THEM, THREATENING TO FALL ONTO HER CHEEKS.

AGAINST HIS BETTER JUDGMENT HE WALKED TOWARDS HER AND TOOK HER HAND IN HIS.

"BELIEVE ME," HE SAID. "THIS IS THE ONLY WAY."

TWO TEARS CASCADED DOWN HER CHEEKS AS HE OPENED THE PALM OF HER HAND, BROUGHT IT UP TO HIS LIPS AND PLACED A DESPERATE KISS ONTO IT.

ALANA ONLY HAD A MOMENT TO SAVOR THIS
FAREWELL BEFORE HE DROPPED BOTH OF
HER HANDS AND RUSHED OUT THE DOOR AS
THOUGH ASHAMED OF HIMSELF.

SHE STAYED THERE FOR A LONG WHILE,
LOOKING BETWEEN THE DOOR WHERE LLEW
HAD LEFT AND THE SUITCASE SITTING OPEN
ON HER BED.

SLOWLY, SHE WIPED THE TEARS FROM HER
EYES, MOVED TO THE OPEN SUITCASE, AND
BEGAN TO PACK.

CHAPTER THREE

AT EXACTLY THREE O'CLOCK, ALANA MOVED AS QUIETLY AS SHE COULD DOWN THE DIMLY LIT STAIRCASE. THE BACK STAIRCASE WAS MUCH NARROWER THAN THE MAIN WINDING ONE WHICH LED OUT OF HER BEDROOM. IT WAS A CHORE TO MOVE BOTH HERSELF AND HER SUITCASE THROUGH IT.

SHE FINALLY MANAGED TO REACH THE DOOR AT THE BOTTOM OF THE STAIRS AND TWISTED IT OPEN. IT REVEALED A LARGE, PRISTINE LOOKING KITCHEN WITH ONE WOOD-BURNING OVEN AND TWO STOVES.

ALANA SEARCHED THIS ROOM UNTIL, FINALLY, SHE FOUND THE BACK DOOR LLEW HAD INSTRUCTED HER TO LEAVE FROM. AS QUICKLY AS SHE COULD, SHE MOVED TOWARDS IT.

"I'D A FEELING HE WOULD SEND YOU OUT THE BACK WAY."

ALANA JUMPED AND LET OUT A SMALL CRY AT THE SOUND OF THE WOMAN'S VOICE. SLOWLY, SHE TURNED AROUND TO SEE A TALL WOMAN MAKING HER WAY TOWARDS HER FROM AN ARCHWAY AT THE FAR END OF THE KITCHEN.

SHE KNEW FROM THE LONG BLONDE HAIR MIXED WITH GRAY AND THOSE BRIGHT

GREEN EYES THAT THIS WAS LLEW'S MOTHER. SHE ALSO KNEW WHAT LLEW SAID ABOUT THE CLAN CALLING FOR ALANA'S BLOOD. PERHAPS HIS MOTHER WAS A PART OF THAT.

ALANA BACKED TO THE DOOR QUICKLY, HOLDING HER SUITCASE AGAINST HER AS A SHIELD.

"THERE'S NO NEED TO BE AFRAID," THE WOMAN SAID. "I WON'T HURT YOU. BUT I NEED TO SPEAK TO YOU QUICKLY. THERE'S NOT MUCH TIME."

"TIME FOR WHAT?" ALANA ASKED SLOWLY LOWERING HER CASE, HER EYES STILL NARROWED SKEPTICALLY.
"THE RITUAL WILL BEGIN AFTER SUNSET," MRS. COUCH SAID. "THE CLAN IS EXPECTING AN AREFOL GIRL TO BE THERE. IT DOESN'T MATTER TO THEM IF YOU ARE KILLED FOR OWAIN'S DEATH OR YOU'RE MADE A CONSORT. EITHER WAY, YOU MUST BE THERE."

"LLEW SAID—"

"LLEW IS WILLING TO TAKE THE PUNISHMENT FOR YOU," SHE SAID.

"THE PUNISHMENT?" ALANA ASKED. SHE FELT HER HEART BEGIN TO BEAT QUICKLY THINKING ABOUT WHAT THAT MIGHT MEAN.

"THEY WILL KILL HIM IF YOU'RE NOT THERE," THE WOMAN SAID.

ALANA FELT HER LEGS BEGIN TO GIVE OUT. SHE PLACED HER HAND ON THE KITCHEN WALL FOR SUPPORT.

"I KNOW HE WANTS TO PROTECT YOU," MRS. COUCH CONTINUED. "I KNOW WHAT YOU MEAN TO HIM BUT...I CAN NOT...I WILL NOT LOSE BOTH MY SONS."

ALANA LOOKED AT THE GROUND TRYING TO THINK OF A RESPONSE, OF SOMETHING SHE COULD SAY THAT WOULD MAKE SENSE. IT WAS STILL TOO MUCH TO PROCESS.

"THE TRUTH IS," MRS. COUCH CONTINUED. "IF YOU GO INTO THAT CIRCLE TONIGHT, I'VE NO IDEA WHAT WILL HAPPEN TO YOU. YOU MIGHT BE KILLED, YOU MIGHT BE GIVEN TO THE CLAN, LLEWELLYN MIGHT FIND SOMEWAY TO SAVE YOU. BUT, I KNOW WHAT WILL HAPPEN IF YOU ARE NOT THERE. I KNOW MY SON WILL DIE."

ALANA LICKED HER LIPS AS SHE LET MRS. COUCH'S WORDS SINK IN. LLEWELLYN KNEW THAT HE WOULD DIE IF SHE DID NOT ATTEND THE RITUAL. WHEN HE TOLD HER TO LEAVE, HE KNEW THAT HE WOULD HAVE TO PAY THE PRICE FOR HER. AND, WHAT'S MORE, HE WAS WILLING TO.

NOW, SHE HAD A CHANCE TO SAVE HIM. EVEN IF SHE DIED IN THE PROCESS, SHE REALIZED IT WAS WELL WORTH THE RISK.

SLOWLY, SHE LOOKED UP FROM THE FLOOR INTO THE EYES OF LLEW'S MOTHER. THE EYES THAT LOOKED SO MUCH LIKE HIS, AND NODDED.

"ALL RIGHT," SHE SAID. "I'LL GO TO THE CEREMONY."

CHAPTER FOUR

ALANA HAD BEEN DRESSED AND PREPARED IN MRS. COUCH'S OWN ROOM. IT WAS LARGER, SHE CLAIMED, THAN ALANA'S BED CHAMBER.

LLEW'S MOTHER HAD PLACED ALANA IN A LONG, WHITE, CHIFFON GOWN WITH BELL SLEEVES. A LONG, DARK BRAID ENCIRCLED HER HAIR AND A CROWN OF RED FLOWERS HAD BEEN WOVEN INTO IT.

ONCE THE OLDER WOMAN WAS SATISFIED, SHE LED ALANA OUT OF THE MANOR TOWARDS THE RUINED CASTLE. IN THE FADING LIGHT OF THE SETTING SUN, ALANA COULD SEE THAT MORE THAN TWO DOZEN PEOPLE WERE ALREADY GATHERED INSIDE THE RING OF STANDING STONES.

MRS. COUCH KEPT ALANA AT A DISTANCE. HIDDEN IN THE SHADOW OF THE MANOR.

"REMEMBER," MRS. COUCH SAID TO HER. "WHEN THE TIME COMES, YOU WILL WALK SLOWLY TOWARDS THE STANDING STONES. THE CLAN MEMBERS WILL MAKE WAY FOR YOU. WHEN YOU REACH LLEWELLYN, REPEAT THE PHRASE I'VE TAUGHT YOU."

"WNEUD GYDA MI FEL BYDDWCH YN," ALANA REPEATED CLUMSILY, THE WELSH WORDS FEELING STRANGE INSIDE HER MOUTH.

LLEW'S MOTHER LOOKED AT HER CRITICALLY.

"CLOSE ENOUGH," SHE SAID FINALLY. "WHEN THE SINGING BEGINS, MAKE YOUR WAY TO THE STANDING STONES."

THEY WAITED WHAT FELT TO ALANA LIKE AN ETERNITY BEFORE THE SUN DIPPED BEHIND THE CLIFFS AND THE FULL MOON BEGAN TO RISE.

WHEN THE CHANTING BEGAN, SIMILAR TO WHAT SHE HAD HEARD ON HER SECOND DAY AT THE MANOR, BUT SOMEHOW VERY DIFFERENT, ALANA'S HEART BEGAN TO POUND INSIDE HER CHEST. ANXIOUS SHIVERS COVERED HER ENTIRE BODY AND SHE FELT ROOTED TO THE SPOT. SUDDENLY, SHE COULD NOT MOVE.

IT TOOK A SHOVE FROM LLEWELLYN'S MOTHER TO FORCE HER FEET FORWARD. SHE WALKED SLOWLY TO HER DESTINATION, FEELING VERY MUCH LIKE A SPOTLESS LAMB BEING LED TO THE SLAUGHTER.

WHEN SHE REACHED THE STANDING STONES, JUST AS MRS. CROUCH HAD SAID, THE CLAN MEMBERS MOVED ASIDE FOR HER. WHEN THEY DID, SHE COULD SEE LLEWELLYN STANDING IN THE MIDDLE OF THE CIRCLE.

AS SOON AS SHE CAUGHT SIGHT OF HIM, HER

heart settled. Even when his face drained of color and his eyes widened in shock, she did not waver in her resolve.

"Alana, what are you doing?" he whispered when she reached him. "I told you to leave."

She did not answer but gave him a small shaky smile. When the chanting reached its end, she dropped to her knees in front of him, just as she had been instructed to do.

"Wneud gyda mi fel byddwch yn."

Once she had uttered the phrase, she looked up at him hoping that he would read what was written in her eyes. Hoping he would realize why she had to do this.

He stared at her a long while and Alana felt her heartbeat quicken once more.

Finally, he grasped her hand in his and pulled her up to her feet. Before she knew what was happening, he pulled her in for a searing, lust filled kiss. There were several yells and whistles from the men in the crowd. It was clear from their chants that they thought

LLEW MEANT TO MAKE HER THEIR CONSORT.

WHEN HE PUSHED ALANA BACK FROM HIM, SHE STEELED HERSELF. SHE HAD PROMISED SHE WOULD ACCEPT WHATEVER FATE LLEW WISHED FOR HER. SHE HAD MEANT WHAT SHE SAID. SHE BELONGED TO HIM, BODY AND SOUL, WHATEVER THAT MEANT.

SHE TOOK A DEEP BREATH AS LLEWELLYN TURNED TO THE CROWD.

"THIS," HE SAID TO THEM IN A LOUD VOICE, "IS MY CHOSEN MATE."

THE CATCALLS AND WHISTLES STOPPED INSTANTLY. A TENSE, PREGNANT SILENCE FELL OVER THE CROWD. EVEN AS ALANA'S HEART JUMPED WITH JOY AT WHAT SHE HAD HEARD, SHE LISTENED TO THE SOUND OF DISAPPROVING WHISPERS FROM THE MEN AROUND HER.

"SHE BELONGS TO ME AND NO ONE ELSE MAY CLAIM HER," HE SAID. "I WILL PROVE THIS TO YOU NOW."

ALANA STOOD FROZEN AS LLEWELLYN MADE HIS WAY OVER TO HER. SHE REMEMBERED WHAT BEING MATED TO HIM MEANT. WHAT SHE WOULD HAVE TO DO.

SHE SWALLOWED HARD AND STEELED HERSELF ONCE AGAIN AS LLEWELLYN TOOK

HER IN HIS ARMS AND KISSED HER FORCEFULLY.

THIS KISS WAS POSSESSIVE, CALCULATED AND HARSH. THERE WAS NOTHING WARM OR LOVING ABOUT IT. EVEN SO, ALANA OPENED HER MOUTH TO WELCOME HIM. SHE COULD FEEL THE MAN SHE DESIRED BEHIND THIS HARDENED FACADE.

HE PULLED AWAY FROM HER AND WHISPERED IN HER EAR.

"I CAN'T BE GENTLE IN FRONT OF THEM," HE SAID. "THEY NEED TO SEE THAT I AM IN CONTROL OF YOU. THEY NEED TO SEE THAT I AM A LEADER. DO YOU UNDERSTAND?"

HE PULLED BACK SLIGHTLY AND SEEMED TO WAIT UNTIL SHE NODDED HER HEAD 'YES'.

HE LOOKED AT HER ANOTHER MOMENT, EYES SOFT, AND NODDED IMPERCEPTIBLY BEFORE STEPPING BACK AGAIN. SHE COULD SEE THIS HARD, COLD FACADE CREEP OVER HIS FACE ONCE MORE. AND, SHE UNDERSTOOD, HE WOULD BE PLAYING A ROLE FOR HIS AUDIENCE. SHE HAD TO PLAY HERS AS WELL.

"ON YOUR KNEES," HE SAID FIRMLY.

ALANA CAST HER EYES DOWN AND DID AS SHE WAS TOLD. SHE WATCHED AS LLEW

SLOWLY UNBUTTONED HIS TROUSERS AND PULLED OUT HIS LONG, SLENDER MEMBER, ONLY HALF HARD.

HE PRESSED IT TO HER LIPS AND, LOOKING UP AT HIM, SHE UNDERSTOOD WHAT HE WANTED. TENTATIVELY, SHE LICKED HIS LENGTH BEFORE SLOWLY ENCOMPASSING HIM FULLY.

AS SOON AS SHE DID, HE PRESSED HIS HANDS INTO HER HAIR AND FORCED HER TO SUCK AND LICK HIM UNTIL HE WAS FULLY HARD AND HIS MEMBER WAS LACED WITH THE BEGINNINGS OF THICK JUICES.

SHE GASPED WHEN HE TUGGED AT HER HAIR AND PULLED HER HEAD UP. LOOKING INTO HIS EYES, SHE PULLED HER MOUTH AWAY FROM HIM AND ALLOWED HIM TO GRAB HER HANDS AND LIFT HER TO HER FEET.

"NOW, STRIP," HE SAID. "SLOWLY, SO THAT I CAN WATCH YOU."

SHE CAUGHT A GLIMPSE OF THE CROWD NOW MURMURING TO EACH OTHER AND, SUDDENLY, SHE COULD NOT MOVE. SHE HAD NEVER UNDRESSED, EVEN IN FRONT OF WOMEN BEFORE. SHE DID NOT KNOW HOW SHE WAS GOING TO REVEAL HERSELF TO A CROWD OF MORE THAN TWENTY-FOUR ONLOOKERS, MOST OF THEM MEN.

She gasped when a hand grabbed hard at her wrist, twisting it. Llewellyn brought her to him, his eyes hard.

"Do you want to make me angry?" he asked.

"N-no sir," she said timidly.

"Then do as I say," he let go of her wrist and shoved her to the middle of the circle. She looked at him and his eyes softened. She could see the facade falling away.

Keeping her eyes trained on his, she slowly reached behind herself and untied the clasp of her dress. Just as slowly, she pushed the dress off of her shoulders and allowed it to skim over her hips as it fell to the ground.

Llewellyn stroked himself just as slowly as she undressed. Lazily running a hand over his member as his eyes roamed over every inch of her smooth, tan skin.

When her bra and panties had been discarded, she shivered against the slight breeze in the air, very aware that she was standing completely naked, completely vulnerable in front of these men.

"COME TO ME," LLEWELLYN SAID CROOKING HIS FINGER AND BECKONING HER TO HIM.

HE TOOK HER HAND AND LED HER TO THE BACK OF THE CIRCLE WHERE A ROUGH CHAIR CARVED FROM ROCK STOOD. LLEWELLYN TOOK HIS SEAT ON THIS THRONE AND, ONCE MORE, BECKONED ALANA TO HIM. SHE MOVED TO HIM AND STOOD BY HIS SIDE.

HE GRABBED HOLD OF HER WAIST AND FORCED HER MOUTH DOWN ONTO HIS ONCE MORE. ONCE MORE, HE MOVED HIS MOUTH TO HER EAR.

"DON'T BE AFRAID," HE SAID.

WITH THAT, HE GRABBED HOLD OF HER WAIST AND FORCED HER ONTO HIS KNEE. HIS MOUTH CLAMPED HARD DOWN ONTO HER NECK AS IT SUCKED AND BIT AGAINST HER. HIS HANDS GROPED HER BREASTS ROUGHLY BEFORE MOVING BETWEEN HER LEGS.

SHE CRIED OUT WHEN HIS FINGERS FOUND HER CLIT AND BEGAN TO CIRCLE HER OVER AND OVER AND OVER AGAIN BRINGING HER TO THE BRINK OF ECSTASY THEN FALLING BACK.

"WHO DO YOU BELONG TO?" LLEWELLYN ASKED LOUDLY ENOUGH THAT THE CROWD, STILL WATCHING COULD HEAR. HE TOUCHED

HER AGAIN JUST WHERE SHE WANTED, NEEDED TO BE TOUCHED.

"Y-YOU," SHE SAID DESPERATELY. "I BELONG TO YOU."

"WILL YOU EVER BELONG TO ANYONE ELSE?" HE ASKED. BEFORE SHE COULD ANSWER, HE TOOK TWO FINGERS AND SHOVED THEM ROUGHLY INSIDE OF HER.

"NO-NO. NO ONE ELSE," SHE SAID. HIS FINGERS MOVED INSIDE OF HER AND SHE CRIED OUT AGAIN AS HE HIT AGAINST HER DESIRE.

"OH, GOD!" SHE SAID. AS SOON AS SHE DID, HE REMOVED HIS FINGERS FROM HER AND SHE LET OUT A WHIMPER OF PROTEST. BUT, BEFORE HER HEART COULD SINK IN DISAPPOINTMENT, HE PULLED HER ROUGHLY BACK TO HIM AND MOVED BENEATH HER.

BEFORE SHE COULD READY HERSELF, HE THRUST INSIDE OF HER WITH ALL THE STRENGTH HE HAD.

SHE CRIED OUT, FIRST IN PAIN. THE FOREIGN OBJECT MOVING AGAINST HER CAUSED A STABBING SENSATION IN PLACES SHE DID NOT EVEN KNOW SHE HAD.

SUDDENLY, HE REACHED AN ARM OUT TO COVER HER BREAST AND, BRIEFLY, SHE

STOPPED MOVING.

"RELAX," HE SAID. "IT'S JUST ME. I'M HERE. I WON'T HURT YOU."

TAKING A DEEP BREATH, SHE TURNED HER NECK TO LOOK AT HIM. HIS EYES WERE SOFT AGAIN. SLOWLY, SHE NODDED HER UNDERSTANDING.

AS SOON AS SHE DID, HIS EYES HARDENED ONCE MORE AND HE BEGAN FORCEFULLY THRUSTING INTO HER. SHE TOOK A DEEP BREATH AND, FOR THE FIRST TIME, FELT AN INCREDIBLE, INDESCRIBABLE PLEASURE BEHIND THE PAIN.

LLEWELLYN WAS INSIDE OF HER. HE WAS PART OF HER. THAT THOUGHT ALONE CAUSED A FLOOD OF WETNESS TO FLOW TO HER CENTER, EASING HIS THRUSTS. WHEN HE TOOK ONE HAND AND WRAPPED IT AROUND HER WAIST, SHE GASPED AS HE BEGAN, ONCE AGAIN TO FINGER HER CLIT.

"ONCE AGAIN, MY LITTLE AREFOL," HE SAID. "WHO DO YOU BELONG TO?"

THE PRESSURE BUILDING INSIDE OF HER FROM HIS POWERFUL THRUSTS MIXED WITH THE TANTALIZING TEASING OF HER CLIT WAS ALMOST ENOUGH TO RENDER HER SPEECHLESS. THEN, SHE LET OUT A SCREAM WHEN HIS FREE HAND SLAPPED AGAINST HER

BOTTOM.

"ANSWER ME," HE GROWLED. "WHO DO YOU BELONG TO?"

"I BELONG TO YOU," SHE SAID BREATHLESSLY. "I'LL ALWAYS BELONG TO YOU."

"GOOD," HE PURRED. "NOW COME FOR ME, MY PRETTY LITTLE AREFOL."

WITH ANOTHER FLICK OF HIS FINGER AGAINST HER CLIT AND A FORCEFUL THRUST INSIDE OF HER, SHE CAME SCREAMING AND PANTING AND MAKING SOUNDS SHE DID NOT KNOW SHE COULD MAKE.

HE FOLLOWED SOON AFTER PRESSING HER FAST AGAINST HIS NAKED CHEST CURSING INTO HER EAR.

WHEN IT WAS DONE, HE HELD HER THERE FOR SEVERAL MOMENTS. SHE LISTENED TO HIS BREATHING AND FELT IT SYNC IN TIME WITH HER OWN. FINALLY, HE PRESSED A KISS TO HER NECK AND MOVED HIS LIPS TO HER EAR.

"I LOVE YOU," HE WHISPERED TO HER.

ALANA HAD NO CHANCE TO ANSWER BEFORE HE PUSHED HER FROM HIM, FOLDED HIS MEMBER BACK INTO HIS TROUSERS AND

MOVED TO THE MIDDLE OF THE CIRCLE ONCE MORE.

"YOU ARE WITNESSES," HE SAID. "I HAVE TAKEN MY MATE. SHE IS MINE AND I AM HERS."

THERE WAS SILENCE WITHIN THE WAITING GROUP FOR WHAT SEEMED LIKE FOREVER. ALANA FEARED FOR A MOMENT THAT IT HADN'T BEEN ENOUGH. THAT THE CLAN WOULD DEMAND THAT THEY BOTH DIE.

THEN, OUT OF SOMEWHERE NEAR THE BACK, A VOICE CALLED OUT.

"SHE IS YOURS FOREVER!"

MORE VOICES SLOWLY BEGAN TO REPEAT THE SAME MANTRA. ALANA LOOKED UP AT LLEWELLYN, WHO, APPARENTLY SATISFIED, SMILED DOWN AT HER.

THEN, QUICKLY, HE MOVED HIS HANDS BENEATH HER AND PICKED HER UP IN HIS ARMS AS THOUGH SHE WERE A BRIDE ON THE WAY TO HER HONEYMOON SUITE.
THE GROUP FELL SILENT AS THEY LEFT THE SAME WAY ALANA HAD ENTERED. WHEN SHE EXITED THE CIRCLE, SHE HEARD A LOUD CRY OF JUBILATION AND SOON, LAUGHING VOICES AND MUSIC ACCOMPANIED THEM.

SOMEHOW, THEY HAD DONE IT. LLEWELLYN

HAD ASSERTED HIS WILL. HIS PLACE AS THE CLAN LEADER WOULD NEVER BE QUESTIONED AGAIN.

HE CARRIED HER ALL THE WAY UP THE STAIRS UNTIL THEY REACHED HER BEDROOM. ONCE THERE, HE SET HER DOWN GENTLY, HER NAKED FORM LYING STARKLY AGAINST THE SATIN SHEETS.

"DID I DO OK?" SHE ASKED WITH A PLAYFUL SMILE ON HER FACE.

"YOU WERE PERFECT," HE SAID GENTLY. "THEY TOOK TO YOU IMMEDIATELY."

"HOW DO YOU KNOW?" SHE ASKED.

"BECAUSE THEY DIDN'T TRY TO KILL YOU," HE SAID. "IT WAS CLEAR AS SOON AS YOU ENTERED, ALMOST EVERY MAN IN THAT CIRCLE WANTED YOU. ALL THOUGHTS OF SPILLING YOUR BLOOD FOR OWAIN'S DEATH DISAPPEARED THE MOMENT THEY SAW YOU."

"I BET THEY WEREN'T TOO HAPPY WHEN THEY FOUND OUT THEY WOULDN'T GET TO HAVE ME," SHE SAID.

"THEY'LL LIVE WITH IT," HE SAID. "IF THEY DON'T...THEY KNOW THE CONSEQUENCES OF UPSETTING THE CLAN LEADER."

HE BENT DOWN AND, ONCE MORE KISSED

her lips. Looking at her now, stretched out and naked and vulnerable, he could hardly believe that she was his. That this beautiful woman would belong to no one but him from now on.

"So, what happens now?" she asked.

"Now," he said removing his trousers and joining her on the bed. "I get to take my wife without an audience."

"Sounds good to me," she said with a smile.

And, as her husband moved against her. As he kissed, touched worshiped every inch of her body, Alana knew that, at last, she had found home.

www.ingramcontent.com/pod-product-compliance
Lightning Source LLC
Chambersburg PA
CBHW032340201025
34265CB00045BA/1187